0709072

THE LIBRARY OF FUTURE WEAPONRY™

NAVAL WARFARE OF THE FUTURE

Richard Mueller

The Rosen Publishing Group, Inc., New York

To Robert H. Mueller

Published in 2006 by The Rosen Publishing Group, Inc.
29 East 21st Street, New York, NY 10010

First Edition

Library of Congress Cataloging-in-Publication Data

Mueller, Richard, 1946-
Naval warfare of the future/Richard Mueller.—1st ed.
    p. cm.—(The library of future weaponry)
Includes bibliographical references and index.
ISBN 1-4042-0526-8 (library binding)
1. Sea-power—Juvenile literature. 2. Warships—Juvenile literature. I. Title. II. Series.
V109.M84 2006
359--dc22

                                                                    2005016874

Manufactured in the United States of America

On the cover: A preliminary design of the littoral combat ship.

CONTENTS

INTRODUCTION

0630, April 4, 2032, Indian Ocean

Alarm bells sound aboard the aircraft carrier *Benjamin Franklin*. Four strike aircraft have been detected in the area. The sailors of the *Franklin* and its surrounding escort vessels rush to their battle stations.

Two of the *Franklin*'s Strike-Angel fighters streak toward the four attackers. Aboard the *Franklin*, all of the Phalanx 9 nitrogen-cooled Gatling guns spring to life, ready to fire. The escorts activate their surface-to-air missile batteries and move into the most effective formation to repel an air attack.

On the bridge of the *Franklin*, Admiral Phenow and Captain Wachtel watch the threat board. "It's a decoy," the admiral says. "The real attack will come from somewhere else."

The captain nods. He has worked through this problem on the holographic simulator dozens of times, but this is the first time he is in it for real. He looks around him. Everyone is reacting perfectly, doing the jobs they have been trained to do. He has confidence in his team.

The Strike-Angels fire first. Their missiles scream toward the intruders, who release their own missiles and speed off. Fireballs erupt in the sky as a number of missiles collide. Two of the Strike-Angel missiles slip past, catching and downing two of the attacking aircraft. The other two enemy planes drop to sea level, hit their afterburners, and race for home.

"So much for the decoys," the captain says. As he speaks, a voice comes over his headset: "We have multiple cruise missile launches out of the seabed 120 miles to the north."

Captain Wachtel steps into the PsyWar room. Two telekinetic techs are on duty, watching the screens. The techs operate unmanned missile intercept vehicles by thought alone. Not being psy, Captain Wachtel doesn't understand how they can do it, but he is grateful that they can. His ships and his men might just depend on them.

The techs concentrate. They guide the intercept vehicles toward the enemy al-Tar missiles and mentally command them to unleash their antimissiles at the target. Of the twenty missiles that have left their barns on the seabed, eight are hit. They crash harmlessly into the sea.

Next, a Sea Skua helicopter from the *Franklin* drops in behind the enemy missiles and shoots down four more with its laser. Unfortunately, eight enemy missiles get away. Then the Sea Skua peels off. It is getting too close to the fleet's deadly antiaircraft batteries.

As a last defense, the fleet opens up with its missiles and laser-tracking Gatlings, filling the sky with destruction. Seven of the remaining cruise missiles are shredded. As smoking rubble rains down on the ships, the radar operators pronounce the skies clear. "Anyone hit?" asks the admiral.

"One missile got through and struck the *Burbank*. It's got a few casualties, but the fire's under control, and the damage won't affect its speed."

The admiral looks out at the smoke trailing from the damaged cruiser. "Have we located the base those fighters came from?"

"Yes, sir."

"Let's hit 'em back."

What you have just read never took place, but something like it may happen in the future. Weapons and strategies that may sound like science fiction are being developed by the world's navies right now. Those developments will determine the future of naval warfare. Read on to learn more.

CVN 76

SHIPS AND THE SEA

The first navies were designed to carry armies to foreign shores or to defend domestic shores from invaders. Early on, that meant carrying marines and archers aboard the same ships that carried the army. Specialized vessels called warships were later developed to sink transport vessels and fight other warships. First with outfitted catapults, then with cannons, and finally with heavy naval guns and torpedoes, warships grew bigger and more complex. The result was that nations were able to extend their power across the globe. The most powerful nations began to create great empires of overseas colonies.

FIGHTING FOR CONTROL OF THE SEAS

Over time, admirals realized how important it was to interfere with the enemy's sea trade. If food and raw materials are kept from reaching the adversary, his or her war effort starves.

A squadron of torpedo bombers prepare for takeoff aboard the carrier USS *Enterprise* (CV6) during the Battle of Midway on June 4, 1942. The *Enterprise* helped repel an attack by the Japanese navy on Midway Island, a major U.S. military base. The victory, which resulted in the destruction of four Japanese aircraft carriers, was a major turning point in World War II.

Island nations such as Britain and Japan are particularly vulnerable to this tactic, which is called interdiction. The struggle for control of the oceans has led to many famous battles, such as those at Lepanto, Trafalgar, Jutland, and Midway.

However, control of the sea often relies solely on the threat of force. A warship can present such a threat by patrolling and showing its flag on distant waters. In peacetime, potential enemies are reminded that powerful ships have the ability to interrupt trade and bring a nation's economy to its knees.

WHERE NAVIES GO

The seas fall under three general areas: littorals, deep water, and choke points.

ALFRED THAYER MAHAN

In 1890, Alfred Thayer Mahan wrote a book called *The Influence of Sea Power Upon History, 1660–1783*. At the time, Mahan was a professor at the United States Naval War College in Newport, Rhode Island. His book argued that the traditional tactic of commerce raiding (sinking the enemy's merchant ships) was no longer the way to win a war. He believed a navy needed to concentrate on beating the enemy's armed fleet in order to win command of the sea. His ideas were eagerly accepted by navies and naval officers all over the world.

Mahan's ideas formed much of the basis for the naval arms race between Britain and Germany prior to World War I. His ideas also motivated nations to open naval academies where imaginary future wars were played out and studied.

Today, at the Naval War College where Mahan taught, these computer simulations of war, known as war games, teach naval officers what to expect before they get into actual combat.

The littorals are the coastal zones, from the beaches out to deep water (those depths where fleet submarines may operate freely). They also include rivers and harbors. They have special problems because ships near the littoral zones may be attacked from land bases as well as from the sea. Also, shallow waters are easier to plant with naval mines or to defend with small, fast motorboats (also called "swarming boats") or coastal submarines.

The *Sea Fighter* (FSF-1) is a high-speed vessel designed to operate in coastal regions, which are also known as littorals. The *Sea Fighter*, pictured above during construction on February 4, 2005, is an experimental ship. It will test features that the navy hopes to incorporate into future projects such as the littoral combat ship.

Deep water refers to areas of the ocean away from the land, with more room to maneuver and more water to hide in, especially for submarines. Ships used to be able to disappear in the deep water, but now with advanced radar, sonar systems, and spy satellites, concealment becomes next to impossible.

The choke points are those narrow passages of water between landmasses where freighters and tankers have to pass as they transport their goods. They may be man-made (like the Panama or Suez canals) or natural (like the Strait of Gibraltar or the English Channel). The nation that controls a choke point controls the trade running through it.

THE ELEMENTS OF A WARSHIP

Ships are designed with their missions in mind. The three traditional components of a warship are protection, firepower, and speed—though now we add modularity, survivability, and signature reduction as well.

Protection

Protection used to mean armor, watertight compartments, strong construction materials, and tonnage. (The tonnage of a ship is not its actual weight, but the weight of the amount of water that it displaces.) For the most part, armor is a thing of the past. Strong construction materials and watertight compartments offer the most reliable protection. These factors are continually being improved upon.

Sometimes, fixing one problem causes another. In the 1970s, to reduce weight and keep ships from becoming top-heavy, navies started to build ships out of aluminum instead of steel. The United States Navy's Fact Files reveal that America changed this practice in 1975, when the cruiser USS *Belknap* collided with the aircraft carrier USS *John F. Kennedy*. *Belknap* suffered severe damage and casualties because of its aluminum structure. After that, most future surface warships returned to steel construction.

The British learned this same lesson during the Falklands War in 1982. Aluminum has a lower melting point than steel; when hit by cruise missiles, British ships built out of aluminum caught fire and melted.

THE ABCDE OF WARSHIPS

A — Aircraft carriers (CV or CVN)

The standard abbreviation for naval aircraft is V, which is why a nuclear aircraft carrier is a CVN (C=carrier, V=aircraft, N=nuclear). These floating air bases are huge, expensive, and vulnerable. Their fighting power is provided by the aircraft they carry.

B — Battleships (BB)

These fire-belching castles of steel are now extinct. No battleships exist except for those that have been turned into monuments.

C — Cruisers (CG or CGX)

Cruisers are used to scout far ahead of the fleet and raid enemy commerce. They also protect the battle line. These large, fast ships armed with guns and missiles are the successors of the battleships.

D — Destroyers (DD or DDX)

Originally developed to protect battleships from torpedo boats, they are smaller than cruisers but able to fulfill almost any task that a cruiser can.

E — Escort vessels including the littoral combat ship (LCS) and frigates (FFG)

The U.S. Navy is phasing out the frigates and replacing them with new multimission ships, such as the littoral combat ship, which can handle many different types of naval tasks.

Firepower

Firepower is the battery of the warship, including guns, missiles, aircraft, and torpedoes. In the future, firepower may include battle lasers or other directed energy weapons.

Speed

Ships that can reach their destinations quickly are harder to hit. In diesel-powered ships, there is a trade-off with range (the distance a vessel can travel on a full supply of fuel), because the faster they go, the more fuel they burn. With nuclear-powered ships, this isn't such a problem.

Modularity

Modularity is the ability to switch out weapons, aircraft, and equipment. Prepackaged collections of specialized gear are called modules. They can turn a basic hull into a specific type of warship. A module can usually be switched out in three days at a naval base.

Survivability

The ability to stay afloat and fight while you're under attack depends on compartmentalization, damage control, and the presence of medical personnel to treat injured sailors. It also includes wetting-down systems to wash nuclear fallout off the ship and close-range weapons to deal with speedboats, aircraft, and missiles.

A Tactical Tomahawk cruise missile is launched from the destroyer USS *Stethem*. The Tactical Tomahawk became part of the navy's arsenal in 2004. An improved version of earlier cruise missiles, it can be programmed in-flight to change its course and strike alternate targets. It also carries a TV camera onboard that allows commanders to view the target and surrounding area.

Signature Reduction

Signature reduction is the ability to be smaller and less visible on radar, sonar, and other instruments of detection. Stealth technology, which erases a ship's or aircraft's electronic signature, is the ultimate in signature reduction.

AIRCRAFT CARRIERS

An aircraft carrier is a floating, fast-moving airfield. Part of its mission is to prevent wars. The presence of so many airplanes capable of reaching the enemy quickly often discourages an enemy from attacking. In wartime, it provides what the navy's Fact Files calls "a credible, sustainable, independent forward presence." Whenever there is a crisis, the first question is, where are the carriers?

CREATION OF CARRIERS

The U.S. Navy began experimenting with flying planes on and off of battleships and cruisers in the First World War (1914–1918). This led to the development of aircraft carriers. Since then, they have built larger and larger aircraft carriers, as shown on the table on the next page.

GROWTH OF CARRIERS

Carrier	Year Completed	Weight	Capacity
USS *Langley* (CV 1)	1922	14,000 tons	36 aircraft
USS *Hornet* (CV 8)	1941	25,000 tons	96 aircraft
USS *Nimitz* (CVN 68)	1975	91,000 tons	90 aircraft
USS *Stennis* (CVN 74)	1998	101,000 tons	86 aircraft

From *Conway's All the World's Fighting Ships*

Initially, carriers were designed so that their planes could scout ahead to warn the fleet of approaching enemy vessels. By World War II (1939–1945), these planes were also sent on missions to attack the enemy. World War II quickly developed into a carrier war.

THE MODERN CVN

The modern aircraft carrier is nuclear powered; is able to steam at speeds in excess of 30 knots (34.5 miles per hour, or 56 kilometers per hour); and is protected by guns and missiles, as well as its own aircraft and fleet of escort vessels. The U.S. Navy currently has ten nuclear aircraft carriers (CVN), an eleventh under construction, and two more planned. Two conventional aircraft

The USS *Ronald Reagan* (CVN 76) steams through the Pacific Ocean on June 29, 2005. The *Ronald Reagan* is the newest carrier in the navy, joining the fleet in 2003. The carrier is the length of three football fields and weighs 101,000 tons. It can carry over eighty aircraft and 3,200 sailors.

carriers (CV), the USS *John F. Kennedy* and the USS *Kitty Hawk* are still with the fleet, though *Kitty Hawk* is more than forty years old.

Each ship has about eighty-five aircraft formed into a wing. If you don't count the helicopters and reconnaissance and tracker aircraft, the core of the wing is the two fighter/attack squadrons.

NAVAL FIGHTERS

The F-14 Tomcat, which has been in use since 1970, is in the process of being replaced by the F/A-18 E/F Super Hornet. According to the navy's Fact Files, the last Tomcats should be replaced by 2007.

An F/A-18E Super Hornet touches down on the USS *Ronald Reagan* on May 10, 2005. The aircraft is part of the Fighting Redcocks unit of the U.S. Navy's Strike Fighter Squadron 22. The first Super Hornet entered service in 2002. They are expected to remain the navy's primary attack aircraft well into the twenty-first century.

The Super Hornet costs $57 million, which is about $20 million more than a F-14 Tomcat. It has a combat range (the distance a plane can carry a load of bombs or rockets to a target and return) of 1,275 nautical miles (2,363 km). It can fly at Mach 1.8 at a maximum altitude of 50,000 feet (15,240 meters). The E model carries a crew of one, while the F carries a crew of two. Both models are armed with a Vulcan 20-mm cannon and various air-to-air missiles, bombs, mines, and air-to-ground rockets. The Super Hornet is likely to be around for many years. The Tomcat has been in service for more than thirty years, and the Super Hornet will likely last that long, too.

Any upgrades in the strike aircraft will probably be gradual. You will almost certainly not see antigravity engines, Star Trek phasers, or Star Wars blasters. Improvements in weapons, flight performance, and electronics and control systems will be added as they are developed.

THE PARTS OF A CARRIER

Simply put, the aircraft carrier consists of a body full of propulsion machinery (the rudder, engines, and boilers), fuel, ammunition, and living quarters under two flat decks. The lowest deck is the hangar deck, where aircraft are refueled, rearmed, and repaired. The top deck is the flight deck. To move the planes from the hangar deck to the flight deck, there are two or three large elevators.

Takeoff from the flight deck is accomplished by flinging planes into the air by means of steam catapults. An angled strip provides the limited runway surface. On landing, a tailhook, dropped by the pilot, snags arresting wires stretched across the deck. A tall structure called the island (always on the right side of the ship if you face toward the front of the ship) contains the bridge, from which the ship is commanded.

While a World War II carrier would mount hundreds of heavy and light antiaircraft guns, the modern carrier mounts just two Sea Sparrow missile launchers and three Phalanx 20-mm guns.

A modern nuclear aircraft carrier of the USS *Nimitz* class displaces about 100,000 tons of water when fully loaded and has a flight deck the length of three football fields. It takes

A 700-ton section of the aircraft carrier USS *George H. W. Bush* (CVN 77) is lowered into place in a shipyard in Newport News, Virginia, on March 8, 2005. The ship is expected to join the navy's fleet in 2009. The *George H. W. Bush* will be the last of the *Nimitz*-class carriers. Future carriers will be part of the CVN-21 (21st-century Aircraft Carrier) class.

about six years to build a *Nimitz*-class carrier. These carriers are also very expensive, costing about $4.5 billion to build each one. Compare that price tag to a World War II aircraft carrier of the *Essex* class, which costs about $30 million.

THE CARRIER TASK FORCE

A carrier task force is grouped around a modern nuclear aircraft carrier. This force consists of a screen of cruisers and destroyers (ships with full batteries of offensive and defensive weapons) and one or more hunter-killer submarines. The basic strategy is very simple. Assuming that any attack will be aimed specifically

THE PHALANX

During the American Civil War (1861–1865), Dr. Richard Jordan Gatling invented a primitive machine gun with multiple rotating barrels. The latest ancestor of that weapon is the Phalanx, the U.S. Navy's close-in defense gun. As the navy's Fact Files explain, "Phalanx is the only deployed, close-in weapon system capable of autonomously performing its own search, detect, evaluate, track, engage and kill assessment functions." In plain English, that means if you're in range and the Phalanx decides you're the enemy, you're probably already dead.

The latest models can fire 4,500 rounds per minute. Each gun carries 1,550 20-mm rounds, which means it can shoot off its entire ammunition supply in twenty seconds. The versatile Phalanx can target antiship missiles, aircraft, speedboats, helicopters, and surface mines.

at the carrier, the first job of any defense will be to protect the carrier. Next, each ship will protect itself and the other escorts.

Although the carrier provides the greatest offensive punch, the escorts are also armed and dangerous. Cruisers and destroyers can use Tomahawk cruise missiles to hit distant targets. In major operations like the recent wars in Iraq and Afghanistan, the escorts helped deliver major offensive strikes.

Due to its fighter, strike, and reconnaissance aircraft, a carrier is able to project its power far inland anywhere on the globe. However, carriers are huge and expensive, and many naval experts ask whether the carrier era is ending.

POWER SOURCES OF THE FUTURE

A ship has to create huge amounts of energy in order to operate. The energy, created by the power plant, is used almost entirely

The aircraft carrier USS *John F. Kennedy* and the destroyer USS *Spruance* receive fuel from the USS *Seattle* during training exercises in the Atlantic Ocean in June 2004. Support ships such as the *Seattle* are a critical part of the carrier task force. Without a ship to replenish fuel supplies, carriers and other warships would be limited in how far they could travel from a naval base.

by the engine to propel the ship forward. However, in the future, the energy created by the power plant may be used for other purposes. For this to happen, the U.S. Navy has to develop a larger source of power. Gordon I. Peterson, senior editor of *Sea Power* magazine, puts it very well: "I contend that the next generation aircraft carrier's value is not going to be in the number of aircraft it carries. The value of that carrier will be the size of its electrical power plant."

Larger power plants will provide the energy to fuel electrical and laser-type high-power weapons aboard the carrier. In essence, the carrier will serve as a mobile source of nuclear power. For the first time, the entire energy output of a ship could by channeled into a superweapon like a huge laser beam or a magnetic levitation railgun. This could be the greatest advance in weaponry since the first cannonball.

CGX AND DDX

Today, the traditional roles of cruiser (CG) and destroyer (DD) are being transferred to new high-use ships. These ships come in two different types: large (CGX) and intermediate (DDX). They are able to carry out almost any type of mission anywhere. Their weaponry is impressive and includes rapid-fire 5-inch guns, Phalanx Gatlings, cruise and antiaircraft missiles, and antisubmarine armament.

BEFORE CGX and DDX

Surface warships (battleships, cruisers, and destroyers) were the most powerful ships on the seas until December 7, 1941. On this date, the Japanese attacked the American naval base at Pearl Harbor. The Japanese navy used aircraft carriers to devastate the American fleet. In the future, aircraft carriers would be the strike weapon of choice. Other surface ships would be used in supporting roles: supporting invasions, supporting convoys, or supporting aircraft carriers.

After Pearl Harbor, the next two major naval battles, Coral Sea and Midway, took place between carriers and their aircraft. For the first time, fleets fought without ever seeing each other. The development of the cruise missile further changed how naval battles were fought. The cruise missile gave cruisers and destroyers the ability to strike out to a distance of well over 1,000 miles (1,600 km).

THE CRUISER

The cruiser originally developed from the frigate, a fast-sailing warship. The frigate was designed to support the battle line, scout ahead, and catch enemy merchant ships. In the steam-and-steel period (1861–1914), the cruiser was a speedy warship with smaller but faster-firing guns than a battleship and more armor than a destroyer. Missiles have now replaced many of the guns on cruisers.

THE DESTROYER

After the advent of steam-powered iron vessels, a new threat to battleships and cruisers appeared. This was the self-propelled torpedo. One hit with a torpedo could sink a large and very expensive battleship. Torpedoes were carried by small, fast torpedo boats. To combat the torpedo boat, the torpedo boat destroyer was born. This name was shortened to just "destroyers," and these versatile ships soon took over multiple duties. They

The fast-sailing frigate was one of the earliest warships. Frigates are being phased out of the U.S. Navy and will be replaced with the next generation of cruisers (CGX), destroyers (DDX), and littoral combat ships. Pictured above is the guided missile frigate USS *Vandegrift* (FFG 48), returning to its home port in Yokosuka, Japan.

sank torpedo boats and fought other destroyers. They carried torpedoes themselves and went after enemy cruisers and battleships. When aircraft and submarines came along, they fought them. They laid mines, cleared mines, carried troops and supplies, and served as base ships for seaplanes. They also supported land forces with gunfire. They were, perhaps, the most versatile warships of all time.

GROWING THE CGX AND DDX

It was natural that these two classes of ships (destroyers and cruisers) would survive into the twenty-first century as the CGX and DDX. They will be larger, faster, and stronger than existing cruisers or destroyers. They will also have more complex electronic and computer systems than ships had in the past. Their radar and sonar systems will be state-of-the-art. Another important feature will be the ships' ability to connect to worldwide surveillance and intelligence networks.

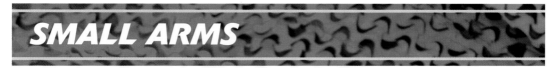

SMALL ARMS

On October 12, 2000, a small craft packed with explosives blew a hole in the side of the USS *Cole* as it was refueling in the Gulf of Aden in the Indian Ocean. The attack, which was organized by the terrorist organization al-Qaeda, killed seventeen U.S. sailors. In order to prevent similar attacks in the future, the navy saw the need to put machine guns and other small arms on ships. The most effective of these is the Mark 38, a 25-mm heavy machine gun that can fire out to a range of 2,700 yards (2,470 m) at 175 rounds per minute. Unlike the Phalanx, the Mark 38 is not computer-run but is fired by a human gunner.

Interestingly, these heavy machine guns are not permanently mounted on ships. They are kept in a weapons pool and assigned to ships that the navy feels might be going into dangerous areas.

The DDX destroyer will eventually replace destroyers currently in the fleet. Above is an artist's depiction of the DDX. One of the advantages of the DDX is that it will require a much smaller crew to operate. The navy also hopes to equip the ship with directed energy weapons, such as high-powered microwaves, that are capable of damaging an enemy ship without destroying it.

AEGIS

Traditionally, the balance between speed, protection, and fire-power meant that you could not increase one without sacrificing the others. A fast ship had to be light and was not as well pro-tected. A ship with heavy guns or armor could not move swiftly. However, these rules have changed. Speed is not as important as it once was because missiles and supersonic aircraft make it nearly impossible for even the fastest ships to elude the enemy. The CGX and the DDX's protection is in guns and electronics. Among the most valuable of these systems is Aegis.

The guided missile destroyer USS *Mason* (DDG 87) is one of many ships in the navy equipped with the Aegis combat system. Aegis has become a popular choice of navies worldwide. Spain, Norway, and Japan already have Aegis-equipped ships in their fleets, while South Korea and Australia plan to add Aegis ships in the future.

The Aegis system (named after the mythological shield of the Greek gods Zeus and Athena) was designed as a total weapon system. This means it is responsible for all aspects of an attack, including detecting, tracking, and striking the target. The heart of the system is a four-megawatt radar capable of keeping track of more than 100 targets at the same time. These targets can be in the air, on the surface, or underwater. While not a weapon itself, it controls the weapons of a ship.

Aegis first went to sea in the *Ticonderoga*–class cruisers. In 1991, it was put in the *Arleigh Burke*–class destroyers. Aegis has been constantly upgraded and improved upon since its inception. It is still the heart of the CGX and DDX and should be around for a long time.

THE FUTURE OF THE CGX AND DDX

In the U.S. Navy, these remarkable ships will be the muscle for eight carrier battle groups and six amphibious groups. They will also operate alone and in pairs to carry out their various missions. The CGX and DDX will be state-of-the-art in surface warships, providing a military presence on the seas for decades to come.

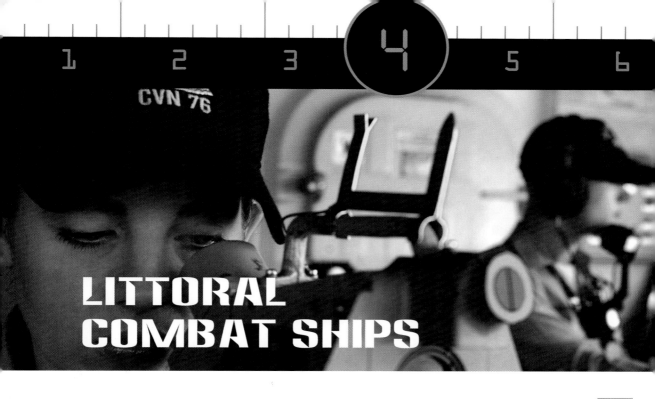

LITTORAL COMBAT SHIPS

The littoral combat ship (LCS) is designed to work close inshore and battle small, fast attack boats. It will also combat diesel-powered coastal submarines and be used to clear mines. It will replace frigates currently in use by the navy, which are slowly being retired from the fleet.

The threat of small attack craft is not new. During the days of wind-powered wooden ships, sailors and marines would often take a ship's rowing longboats into an enemy port. Their mission was to board an enemy vessel at anchor, capture its crew, then sail the ship out to sea.

By the time of the American Civil War, small steamboats with one or two guns would often fight for control of ports or rivers. From these, armored warships known as ironclads and monitors were developed.

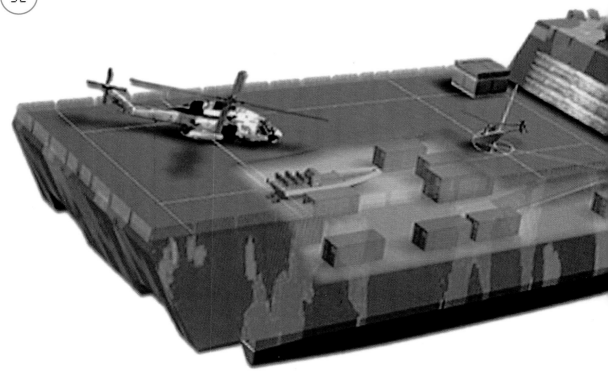

Steam torpedo boats were countered by destroyers, so motor torpedo boats with a few light guns and two or four torpedoes replaced them. Running at speeds of 40 knots (46 mph or 74 km/h) or more, they would strike swiftly, then turn and streak for cover.

The Vietnam War (1965–1973) saw the development of small, fast craft armed with guns, mortars, and flame throwers. They patrolled both rivers and coasts, cutting off enemy supply lines and disrupting operations.

PROTECTING THE COASTS

The new challenge of coastal warfare calls for protecting fleet groups from submarines, mines, and explosive motorboats. It

Two shipbuilding companies, Lockheed Martin and General Dynamics, have been awarded contracts to design and build littoral combat ships. At left is an illustration of the future General Dynamics ship. The two companies' designs for the ships vary slightly, but both versions will be fast, adaptable to many different missions, and manned by a crew of fewer than forty sailors.

also requires craft that can seize and hold a coastline, overwhelming the defenses while an amphibious landing force deploys ashore. This calls for a vessel that can be reconfigured rapidly to suit any task the navy assigns. In the future, this role will belong to the littoral combat ship.

Initially, fifty-six LCSs are planned for construction. These ships will carry modular packages that allow them to reconfigure to meet the needs of the mission. They will also carry Fire Scout light helicopters. The navy plans three Fire Scouts for each LCS. Each Fire Scout will be able to carry eight 2.75-inch Hydra unguided rockets, low-cost guided imaging rockets, the laser-guided Viper Strike unmanned attack aircraft, and a 5-pound (2.3-kilogram) missile called Spike.

Construction of the first ships began in 2005, and the navy will receive the first completed ship in 2007. Britain, France,

The littoral combat ship will carry RQ-8 Fire Scout unmanned aerial vehicles. These pilotless helicopters are capable of vertical takeoff and landing, which is important because the LCS will have limited space for a flight deck. As of July 2005, testing versions of the Fire Scout have flown more than 150 flights. Above is a photograph of a Fire Scout at the Patuxent River Naval Air Station in Maryland.

Italy, and Germany are all very much interested in acquiring their own LCS squadrons.

DESIGNING THE LITTORAL COMBAT SHIP

The design of the LCS will be shaped by the following principles:

Speed

The littoral combat ship will be fast enough to keep pace with the fastest ships in the navy fleet. The plan is for these ships to be able to reach speeds of up to 50 knots (58 mph or 93 km/h).

Connecting to the Network

The LCS will have the advanced technology to link instantly with all levels of command and all forms of surveillance—from orbital satellites and high-flying aircraft to patrol ships, helicopters, and unmanned drones.

Base of Operations

The LCS will serve as a floating base for surface craft or submarines, medium-sized helicopters, or unmanned aerial vehicles. The LCS will also be able to carry sonar buoys that can be dropped overboard. These sonar buoys will be used to locate enemy submarines trying to enter a port or beachhead.

Reduced Manpower

The ship will carry a crew of fewer than forty officers and men. Mission crews will come aboard with various mission modules.

THE REST OF THE FLEET

Submarines, diesel (SS) and nuclear (SSN), are still a commanding presence at sea. Their greatest advantage is stealth—the ability to approach unseen. Surface forces take great pains to discover and kill them. Hunter-killer submarines are specifically designed to destroy other submarines. Ballistic-missile submarines (SSBN) and guided-missile submarines (SSGN) are long-distance strike weapons. Nuclear submarines can remain at sea submerged for long periods of time, giving them the ability to lie silently in wait for enemy ships.

Usually small and light, minecraft are responsible for finding and clearing the enemy mines that lurk under the surface of coastal waters. Minecraft can also plant mines.

The first *San Antonio*–class amphibious warfare vessel began at-sea testing in April 2005. These ships will be able to carry more cargo, troops, and aircraft than existing versions of amphibious vessels could.

Amphibious warfare vessels deliver soldiers to the enemy's coast. The troops often come ashore in large hovercraft known as ground effect machines (GEM), as well as helicopters and traditional landing craft.

The fleet train delivers fuel, food, and ammunition whenever and wherever needed. Most warships are still nonnuclear, and they need replenishment ships to fuel them at sea and form mobile bases around which naval forces may operate. The four *Sacramento*-class replenishment ships carry 177,000 barrels of oil, 2,150 tons of ammunition, 500 tons of dry stores, and 250 tons of refrigerated stores. While warships will be improving in the future, there will always be a need to supply them. Only replenishment ships will be able to carry the heavy loads needed by their fighting cousins.

Quick Change

The LCS will be designed so that reconfiguring a ship from one module to another will take no more than four days.

Modularity

The modular packages of the LCS, which can be switched out in four days, make these ships, according to defense analyst Robert Work, the "Swiss army knife of future naval battle networks."

DIFFERENT MODULES OF THE LCS

The LCS will be able to support many different mission modules, some of which are described in the following pages. These modules allow the LCS to adapt to whatever situation may arise. New modules may be developed to fit new situations, giving the LCS a potentially long life of service at sea.

Modularity is a cost-efficient way of designing ships. If it weren't for the modules, the navy would have to build a separate ship for each type of mission.

Antisubmarine Warfare

The hunting, discovery, tracking, and destruction of enemy submarines involves specialized sonar equipment. It also includes antisubmarine missiles or torpedoes and their launchers. Crewmen complete the package, allowing the LCS to move in fast on a contact and destroy it before the submarine can fire its torpedoes or missiles.

Mine Countermeasures

Finding and destroying undersea mines in coastal areas is of prime concern. Mines can be planted by surface ships, submarines, helicopters, or aircraft. They can be exploded by strong magnets, sound, being hit by a ship, or by remote control from a shore station. Hunting them is a crucial task for the LCS.

Antisurface Warfare

In this module, the emphasis is on guns, cruise missiles, and possibly torpedoes. The LCS would join the new cruisers and destroyers to repel attacks by surface craft (including explosive motorboats). They would also assist them in protecting aircraft carriers, amphibious warships, and replenishment vessels.

Intelligence, Surveillance, and Reconnaissance

In the military, collecting information about the enemy is often known as ISR, which stands for intelligence, surveillance, and reconnaissance. ISR is more successful if it isn't noticed. The LCS may be fitted with surfaces that make it difficult to detect by enemy sonar and radar. The LCS will also be outfitted with sophisticated electronic surveillance equipment. Additions to the crew would include electronics technicians, data analysts, and possibly translators. The LCS would cruise off the enemy coast and gather data while remaining nearly invisible to the enemy.

Homeland Defense

In this module, the LCS would likely carry a boarding party (armed sailors trained to capture a boat or ship by overpowering the crew) and sensors for detecting explosives and gas or nuclear emissions. The LCS and its crew would back up the Coast Guard and Harbor Police in preventing acts of terrorism.

Maritime Intercept

Ships charged with the mission of intercepting and stopping merchant vessels at sea would carry guns and a boarding party. They would also carry two types of nonlethal weapons known as stack blockers and running-gear entanglers. (Nonlethal weapons are discussed in more detail in chapter 6.)

Special Operations Support

This module would move into enemy waters to insert Ranger or SEAL teams and recover them when they had completed their missions. The LCS will also rescue downed pilots and deliver emergency coastal bombardment to support friendly troops. Through it all, it will remain stealthy and unobserved, at least until the moment to open fire.

Logistical Support

Logistics deals with the transportation of materials and personnel. This module will allow the LCS to carry supplies to outlying units and escort replenishment ships through combat zones.

THE *SWIFT*

Another possibility for operations in the coastal areas besides the LCS is the *Swift*.

The USS *Swift*, a high-speed vessel (HSV), is an aluminum-hulled catamaran that was delivered to the navy in August 2003. It is currently serving as a mine warfare command and support ship (MCS). The *Swift* was developed from two earlier ships, the *Joint Venture* and the U.S. Army's *Spearhead*. It took only ten months to build.

The *Swift* prepares for refueling during an exercise named Rim of the Pacific in July 2004. Behind the *Swift* is the mine warfare ship USS *Avenger*. The amazing design of the *Swift* allows it to sail in only 11 feet (3.4 m) of water, even while carrying more than 1.2 million pounds (544,310 kg) of cargo.

According to the navy's Fact Files, the *Swift* is 321.5 feet (98 m) long, can carry 605 tons of cargo, and has a maximum speed of 46 knots (53 mph or 85 km/h). At its normal operating speed of 30 knots (34 mph or 55 km/h), it has a range of more than 4,000 miles (6,440 km). It can carry a small, remotely controlled, unmanned aerial vehicle (UAV) that can be fitted with laser-guided rockets. Two men in a control station serve as the remote crew of the UAV. Predator UAVs armed with Hellfire missiles have already been used in missions against the terrorist organization al-Qaeda and in the wars in Afghanistan and Iraq.

WONDER WEAPONS

Radar (radio detecting and ranging) works by bouncing radio waves off of solid objects. As the radar antenna revolves to scan around the ship, a picture of all surrounding radio-reflective objects appears on a computer screen. Radar can tell you how far away an object is and its size, but it cannot determine how fast an object is moving or in which direction. Speed and course can be calculated by a technician who charts the radar signals.

Sonar (sound navigation and ranging) sends a sound pulse, or ping, through the water to locate submerged objects such as submarines. As the sound bounces off a solid object, it reflects back to a detector. In addition to detecting enemy ships, it can also be used to locate mines. Commercial fishermen even use it to find schools of fish.

The navy is currently testing advanced sonar systems. This photograph shows an experimental sonar workstation aboard the USS *Nicholson* (DD 982). The workstation features four touch screens and increased automation to make it easier to use. Sonar systems such as this one will also reduce the number of sonar technicians needed on board.

Both these systems have been improved since the end of the Second World War and may improve further due to technological advances. It is unlikely that some as yet undiscovered technology will completely replace either of them. Both radar and sonar are here to stay.

ELECTRONIC INTELLIGENCE

It used to be that signal intelligence (SIGINT) analysts studied radio transmissions to determine enemy movements and plans. Now, with satellites, computers, and listening stations, electronic

Information Systems Technician 2nd Class Laresa Buxton makes an adjustment to a console on the aircraft carrier USS *Harry S. Truman* (CVN 75). Technicians such as Buxton help different units in the navy, such as aircraft personnel and intelligence experts, communicate with each other. These communications often rely on satellites to relay data to a receiving station, where it is then passed on to whomever needs it.

intelligence (ELINT) taps in on every type of communication worldwide. ELINT uses number-crunching software and sophisticated computer programs to collect and interpret vast amounts of data. The point is that the more you know about what your enemy is going to do, the better you can prepare for it.

THE HIGH GROUND OF SPACE

In the early 1950s, science-fiction writer Arthur C. Clarke speculated that one day in the near future, a network of communications satellites would tie the world together with knowledge. Soon the potential for surveillance (which is called overlook—the ability to see your opponent's forces from a place of safety) was foremost in the U.S. Defense Department's plans. Now, powerful tele-scopic cameras looking down from orbit can allegedly read a car's license plate or the rank insignia on a soldier's uniform. If you took this book outside, it's a good bet that there are spy satellites that could read this book over your shoulder.

Satellites fly in fixed orbits around Earth, and each looks down on a narrow path. If the navy needs to see something out-side that path, the satellite can be reprogrammed and pushed with retro-rockets into a different orbit so that its cameras can overlook the new target.

Satellite pictures are transmitted to a receiving station, where they are filtered and enhanced through computers. These pic-tures can be in the hands of a military officer in seconds. The

CRACKING THE CODE

Enigma was a German coding machine during World War II that was stolen by Polish agents who then passed it on to the British. Using it, the British (and later the Americans) were able to read German plans and react accordingly. U.S. Navy code-breakers in the Pacific were able to break Japanese codes with the machine.

All countries use secret codes, either for political, military, or busi-ness reasons. Countries also seek to break codes, so they will know what current and potential rivals are planning. New codes, coding programs, and code machines are continually being developed.

problem is that satellites are expensive. Once you get through the ticklish business of putting them into orbit, moving them around is tricky, and they carry only so much fuel for the retro-rockets.

Pioneering experiments with high-altitude aircraft have put flying cameras up at the very borders of space. Anything, anywhere, may be seen, photographed, and attacked.

UNMANNED WAR

Many spy aircraft are being replaced by unmanned aircraft and drones. Typical of the UAVs is the RQ-2A Pioneer. Costing just less than a million dollars to build, the Pioneer is 14 feet (4.3 m) long with a 17-foot (5.2 m) wingspan. It can fly up to 110 mph (177 km/h) at an altitude of 15,000 feet (4,572 m). It has a range of 115 miles (185 km), and transmits pictures back to its mother ship without risking the life of a pilot.

Because a slow, unmanned aircraft may be targeted and shot down, smaller drones are being developed. One that was recently demonstrated zipped over its targets at treetop level carrying three computers and two cameras. It was not much larger than a Frisbee.

THE FUTURE OF SURVEILLANCE

In the future, miniaturization will be key to surveillance of the enemy. Unmanned aircraft will be smaller and faster. These qualities will help the aircraft elude the enemy and complete its mission undetected.

The Global Hawk unmanned aerial vehicle has been used by the U.S. Air Force in the recent wars in Iraq and Afghanistan. Pictured above is the N-1, a version of the Global Hawk designed for the navy. It took flight for the first time on October 6, 2004. In the future, the N-1 will be used for naval surveillance missions.

Consider this possible scenario in the near future: An unmanned aircraft released from a ship, traveling high and at night, crosses a coastline due to be invaded. It drops two dozen preprogrammed drones that fall to 1,000 feet (305 m) and then scatter, sending back to the command ship flawless infrared pictures of enemy positions. Each drone is the size of a human thumb. With its mission accomplished, each drone drops to the ground where camouflage on its plastic skin gives it the appearance of a stone. After the invasion, the surviving drones are collected and readied for the next mission.

Sound far-fetched? It's not. If we can imagine it, we can be sure that someone, somewhere, is designing it right now.

WIZARD WARS

The military is always looking for ways to reduce casualties, especially civilian casualties. The deaths of innocent citizens and the destruction of their homes and communities (known as collateral damage) is one of the most tragic aspects of war. In an attempt to reduce the collateral damage of war, the Joint Non-Lethal Weapons Directorate (JNLWD) was created. Its goal was to find nonlethal ways of waging war and protecting American bases.

WEAPONS THAT DISABLE BUT DO NOT KILL

Active Denial Systems (ADS) are weapons that temporarily affect the senses and stop the enemy without killing him or her. On the lowest level, there are beanbag rounds, tasers, water cannons, and tear and pepper gases. Up a

Master-at-Arms 2nd Class Dave Shull Jr. shoots a nonlethal sting ball grenade from a shotgun aboard the USS *Blue Ridge*. The device is used to warn approaching ships that they should not come any closer. Nonlethal devices and weapons such as this one will be an important part of the future navy.

notch from those weapons are explosive stun weapons and gases that can cause vomiting, hallucinations, fear, or unconsciousness.

The area heat ray is another weapon in the ADS arsenal. It emits a high-energy wave that tricks the pain receptors in the skin. Victims feel as if their flesh is on fire. When the heat ray projector is switched off, the pain vanishes completely—but not the memory of it. Few people would be willing to face the experience twice. Anyone zapped by a heat ray is likely to surrender.

The eyes and ears can also be assaulted. Very bright dazzle lights, low-frequency sound projectors, or even extremely loud music can act as a deterrent to violent conflict. These may seem more like annoyances than real weapons, but if they make the enemy surrender, retreat, feel sick, or simply ruin his or her aim, they are just as effective as lethal weapons.

NONLETHAL WEAPONS OF THE FUTURE

These technologies will be used to protect ships and naval bases from crowds of hostile civilians, rioters, or even enemy troops.

Exhaust Stack Blockers

Surprisingly, in these modern times, pirates have made a come-back. They will board a large merchant ship at sea, rob the safe and the crew's valuables, kill or incapacitate the crew, and abandon the ship, leaving it to steam ahead at full speed. While the police or Coast Guard are busy trying to bring the runaway ship under control, the pirates escape. The exhaust stack blocker is designed to be dropped from a helicopter into the ship's smokestack. Once inside, it expands like a balloon and blocks the air intakes, shutting down the engines. A drifting ship is much easier to board than one running unmanned at full speed.

Running Gear–Entangling Systems

There's nothing that will stop a ship faster than a chain or a line wound around its propellers. Especially useful against merchant vessels, entanglers will wrap strong synthetic netting around a propeller and bring it to a halt.

The USS *De Wert* (FFG 45) passes an antiboat barrier system. Barrier systems are designed to protect anchored ships from attack by small enemy craft. The importance of such protection was demonstrated by the terrorist attack on the USS *Cole* in October 2000. In this attack, a small boat loaded with explosives blew a hole in the side of the unprotected *Cole*, killing seventeen American sailors.

Floating Mine Inflatable Barriers

Surrounding an anchored ship by a barrier designed to keep out floating mines, motorboats, or swimmers is not new. Antitorpedo nets made of steel wires and used by ships called net tenders were used by a number of navies, particularly those of the United States and Great Britain. They were heavy, cumbersome, and generally not portable. But a reusable, inflatable version made of strong plastics could be carried aboard any ship and be ready for use in minutes, protecting against anything moving on the surface.

DE-MINING THE BEACHES

Beaches must be cleared of mines before amphibious forces can land. In order to solve this problem, the U.S. Marines have resurrected a sixty-year-old solution. Before American, British, and Canadian troops landed on the coast of France in the D-day invasion of World War II, American Sherman and British Churchill tanks were modified with unrolling mats and sleds to explode mines hidden in the sand. These hybrids, called funnies, were very successful. Now the marines have adapted the Abrams main battle tank by fitting it with a "mine plow" to unearth and explode buried mines and booby traps. Being heavier than its World War II counterparts, the Abrams should have a better chance of surviving explosions.

LASER BEAMS AS WEAPONS

Besides nonlethal weapons, a number of other technologies are being developed for future warfare. One such technology is the laser. In military applications, lasers can be used to carry far more information than radio waves and can act as targeting systems for weaponry. They can also act as beam weapons themselves.

The beam of a laser can cut through metal, destroy electrical systems, and kill or blind personnel. The principal drawbacks

Seen above is a high-energy laser currently being developed by the U.S. Army. In a test at White Sands Missile Range in New Mexico, the laser successfully tracked and zapped a shell fired from an artillery weapon. Some defense experts believe that weapons such as this one are less than five years away from use in combat.

of the laser are that its electronics can easily be bounced out of alignment. Also, as a beam weapon, it uses a great deal of power, which makes its use in space-based systems very diffi-cult. It takes a power plant the size of an aircraft carrier to fire a beam weapon. You can imagine how difficult it would be to get something that heavy into orbit.

However, as noted in chapter 2, the power plant of a ship might create enough energy to power a laser in the future. It might take a while, but laser weapons are likely to be part of naval warfare.

THOUGHT CONTROL

In the 1982 film *Firefox*, actor Clint Eastwood played a pilot who highjacks a Russian fighter plane that was flown by the use of a "thought control" helmet. In a case of life imitating science fiction, this technology is currently under experimentation. The advantage of this sort of advance is that there would be no delay between the pilot's thoughts and the actions of the plane. As soon as the pilot thinks about firing, the plane fires. The disadvantage is that a pilot must always concentrate on the current mission. If the pilot's mind wanders, the pilot would risk crashing the aircraft or getting shot down by the enemy.

PSYWAR

In 1952, the U.S. Department of Defense, in cooperation with the Stanford Research Institute, began to investigate PsyWar (the use of mind weapons). Over the years, the United States military considered ways mind weapons might be used to influence thoughts, cause temporary or permanent mental or physical illness, or move or affect objects from a distance. When a psychic was allegedly able to bend a spoon, the immediate response was, can he bend the gun barrel of a tank?

However, no one would need to actually bend the barrel of a tank. It would be far easier to block or activate an electronic system, open or close a valve, squeeze shut a hose, or detonate an explosive. The idea is if the mind can reach it and understand it, the mind can change it.

The idea of PsyWar is controversial. Most scientists believe it is unlikely to become a reality. Still, the evidence points to military involvement in the past and no one knows for sure what top-secret projects are currently being worked on.

In the future, if PsyWar becomes a reality, it would usher in a whole new era of warfare. We may wind up worrying as much about weapons of mental disturbance as we do now about weapons of mass destruction.

GLOSSARY

amphibious group Landing ships carrying marines, landing craft, armored vehicles, and helicopters for invading and holding beaches in enemy territory.

barn A small, portable missile launcher that can be activated by remote control.

battle line Warships cruising together in formation.

beanbag rounds Plastic bags full of hard pellets that, when fired at a person, cause a stinging bruise. They are a type of non-lethal weapon.

catamaran A fast craft with twin, side-by-side hulls.

collateral damage Unintended damage to things other than the target.

compartmentalization Consisting of sections, or compartments.

damage control Crewmen who respond to combat damage by fixing necessary systems, putting out fires, and keeping the ship seaworthy.

drone An unmanned aircraft.

holographic simulator A 3-D game program with which tactical problems can be played out.

hull The outer body or shell of a ship.

hunter-killer A type of submarine whose main function is to hunt other submarines.

knot A measure of speed. One knot is equal to one nautical mile per hour.

mach The ratio of the speed of an object to the speed of sound. A plane traveling at mach 2 is traveling twice the speed of sound.

magnetic levitation railgun A device that uses magnetism to cause an object, such as a warhead, to float then move forward at very high speeds.

nautical mile One minute of latitude on Earth's surface, or about 6,080 feet (1,853 m).

retro-rockets Rocket motors used to decelerate or change direction.

stealth The ability of a ship or airplane to avoid detection by the enemy.

taser Weapon that subdues its target with a strong electric shock.

task force A group of ships sailing together for a specific mission.

telekinetic Referring to the ability to move or affect objects from a distance without touching them.

threat board A constantly updated display showing any enemy or unidentified contacts.

FOR MORE INFORMATION

Naval Sea Cadet Corps
2300 Wilson Boulevard
Arlington, VA 22201-3308
(703) 243-6910
Web site: http://www.seacadets.org

United States Naval Academy
121 Blake Road
Annapolis, MD 21402-5000
(410) 293-1000
Web site: http://www.usna.edu

Web Sites

Due to the changing nature of Internet links, the Rosen Publishing
Group, Inc., has developed an online list of Web sites related to the
subject of this book. This site is updated regularly. Please use this
link to access the list:

http://www.rosenlinks.com/lfw/nawf

FOR FURTHER READING

Clancy, Tom. *Carrier: A Guided Tour of an Aircraft Carrier*. New York, NY: Berkley Publishing Group, 1999.

Crawford, Steve. *Twenty-first Century Warships: Surface Combatants of Today's Navies*. St. Paul, MN: Motorbooks International, 2002.

Gaines, Ann Graham. *The Navy in Action*. Berkeley Heights, NJ: Enslow Publishers, 2001.

George, James L. *The U.S. Navy in the 1990s: Alternatives for Action*. Annapolis, MD: Naval Institute Press, 1992.

Ripley, Tim. *Weapons Technology*. New York, NY: Facts on File, 2004.

Sweetman, Jack. *American Naval History*. Annapolis, MD: Naval Institute Press, 1984.

Ullman, Harlan. *In Harm's Way: American Seapower in the 21st Century*. Silver Spring, MD: Bartleby Press, 1991.

Wragg, David. *Carrier Combat*. Annapolis, MD: Naval Institute Press, 1997.

BIBLIOGRAPHY

Alexander, John B. *Winning the War: Advanced Weapons, Strategies and Concepts for the Post 9-11 World.* New York, NY: St. Martin's Press, 2003.

Brown, D.K., and George Moore. *Rebuilding the Royal Navy: Warship Design Since 1945.* Annapolis, MD: Naval Institute Press, 2003.

Burgess, Richard R. "Fire Scout UAV Is Poised as Sensor, Shooter for Littoral Combat Ship." *Sea Power,* Vol. 47, No. 5, May 2004.

Chesneau, Roger, ed. *Conway's All the World's Fighting Ships 1922-1946.* Annapolis, MD: Naval Institute Press, 1982.

English, Adrian. *Battle for the Falklands.* With Anthony Watts. London, England: Osprey Publishing, 1982.

Gardiner, Roger, ed. *Conway's All the World's Fighting Ships, 1947–1982, Part I: The Western Powers.* Annapolis, MD: Naval Institute Press, 1982.

Gray, Randal, ed. *Conway's All the World's Fighting Ships, 1947–1982, Part II: The Soviet Bloc and Non-aligned Nations.* Annapolis, MD: Naval Institute Press, 1982.

Grove, Eric J. *Nato Major Warships: USA and Canada.* London, England: Tri-Service Press, 1990.

Kay, Ian, and Mary Walker. *Jane's Defence Glossary*. Coulsdon, England: Jane's Information Group, 1993.

Kemp, Peter, ed. *The Oxford Companion to Ships and the Sea*. Oxford, England: Oxford University Press, 1988.

Martel, William C., ed. *The Technological Arsenal: Emerging Defense Capabilities*. Washington, DC: Smithsonian Institution Press, 2001.

Peterson, Gordon I. "Building More Effective and Efficient Naval Forces for the Future." *Naval Forces*, Vol. 25, No. 1, February 2004.

Potter, E. B., ed. *Sea Power: A Naval History*. Annapolis, MD: Naval Institute Press, 1981.

Work, Robert. "Small Combat Ships and the Future Navy." *Issues in Science and Technology*, Vol. 21, No. 1, Fall 2004.

INDEX

About the Author

A lifelong student of naval history, Richard Mueller has often written on military and naval subjects. After service in the U.S. Coast Guard, he moved to Hollywood, California, where he wrote for television and film, including for the History Channel series *The Great Ships*. He is a member of the Historical Miniatures Gaming Society, Naval Section.

Photo Credits

Cover artist concept provided to the U.S. Navy courtesy Lockheed Martin Corporation; left corner © Digital Vision/Getty Images; top middle © Photodisc Red/Getty Images; p. 7 and througout U.S. Navy photo by Photographer's Mate 2nd Class Kitt Amaritnant; p. 8 © Bettmann/ Corbis; p. 10 U.S. Navy photo by John F. Williams; p. 14 U. S. Navy photo; p. 17 © U.S. Navy photo by Photographer's Mate 3rd Class Christopher Brown; p. 18 U.S. Navy photo by Photographer's Mate 3rd Class Aaron Burden; p. 20 Photo courtesy of Northrop Grumman Newport News; pp. 22–23 U.S. Navy photo by Photographer's Mate 2nd Class Michael Sandberg; p. 26 U.S. Navy photo by Photographer's Mate 2nd Class John L. Beeman; p. 28 © 1999–2003 Raytheon Company; p. 29 U.S. Navy photo by Photographer's Mate 2nd Class Daniel J. McLain; pp. 32–33 U.S. Navy courtesy General Dynamics; p. 34 U.S. Navy photo by Kurt Lengfield; p. 36 Photo courtesy of Northrop Grumman Ship Systems; p. 41 U. S. Navy photo by Photographers's Mate 1st Class Michelle R. Hammond; p. 43 U.S. Naval research Laboratory; p. 44 U.S. Navy photo by Photographer's Mate Airman Gregory A. Pierot; p. 47 Photo courtesy of Northrup Grumman; p. 49 U. S. Navy photo by Photographer's Mate 1st Class Novia E. Harrington; p. 51 U. S. Navy photo by Paul Farley; p. 53 © (AP Photo/ HO, TRW, Inc.)

Designer: Evelyn Horovicz; Editor: Brian Belval